P9-BZJ-459

HANNAH AND DEXTER
The First Meeting

By Shiela Martina
Illustrated by Najah Clemmons

"HANNAH AND DEXTER: The First Meeting"
By Shiela Martina
Martina Publishing 2008©
All Rights Reserved

Shiela Martina
Hannah & Dexter : The First Meeting / Shiela Martina
SUMMARY : Hannah and Dexter have a very unpleasant first
meeting, but with the help of a singing, strict red-haired teacher,
the two children learn that they have more in common than they
thought.
Audience: Ages 7—12

ISBN-13: 978-0-9799344-0-7
ISBN-10: 0-9799344-0-0

1. School—Juvenile Fiction. 2. Multiculturalism—Fiction.
3. History Projects—Fiction. 4. Teachers—Fiction. 5. Library — Fiction I. Title.

Copyright: Martina Publishing, Inc. 2008
Printed in Hong Kong

Dedication

Author: To my mothers, Jennie, Elflorence, and Freddie Mae Oliver,
who always provide me with what I need and want.
In addition, to the many children (young and old)
that will read this book and grow.

Illustrator: To my beautiful "flowers" (daughters),
may you always be able to "hear your dreams."

Hannah is a fun loving nine-year-old girl who lives in a small town in South Carolina. She lives on the Westside of town with her mother and little brother, Charles. Hannah's father moved to another state after he divorced her mother.

Dexter is a very active nine-year-old boy who also lives in a small town in South Carolina. He lives on the Southside of town with his father, mother, and two sisters, Deana and Debra.

On the first day of school, Hannah walked up to two girls in the hallway and said, "Hi, my name is Hannah. Do you want to be my friends?" The girls willingly agreed. Dexter met up with his friends in the hallway. One of Dexter's friends said, "Hey Dexter show us that move you did on the basketball court yesterday." Dexter was not conscious of Hannah and her friends when he pretended to show off his basketball moves. Hannah was so busy gossiping with her new friends that she did not see Dexter coming toward her. The two collided and it was not a pretty sight.

Dexter's friends defended him. "Hey girl, you need to pay attention to where you're going." Hannah's friends yelled back, "That boy should not be doing basketball moves in the hallway." Hannah and Dexter just stared at each other with mean glances without saying a word. The bell rang and everyone hurried to their classes.

Hannah and Dexter met up in the same class. Their new teacher had red hair and blue/green eyes. She dressed like a 1970's super model with platform shoes, a ruffled tailed skirt, and big fancy bracelets on her arm. Everyone admired the way she spoke nicely and the way she kept her class in order. Her voice was very beautiful and she always sang as the class entered the room and as they exited.

When the class came in on the first day of school and each day after that she sang,

> "Let's start at the very beginning
> The class must be quiet to start
> When you read you begin with A-B-C
> When you learn you begin by listening to me!
> Mmm.

Welcome class. My name is Mrs. Rightover. It's nice to meet all of you."

Mrs. Rightover arranged her students' seats in alphabetical order. To their dislike, Hannah and Dexter were in the same class, sitting right next to each other. Mrs. Rightover had the strictness of an old librarian, because she told her class, "No one is allowed to talk while someone else is talking, to move to another person's desk, nor to talk until you are recognized."

The first day of school, Mrs. Rightover assigned a history project. She clearly explained, "the project is due in 3 weeks and is worth half your final grade." One main requirement was that a group of two people must complete it. Hannah raised her hand and asked, "What does the history project have to be about?" Mrs. Rightover answered, "This project must be about an unforgettable moment in history."

Quickly the class went into a loud buzz with everyone claiming their project partners. "I want you to be my partner, Teresa," Hannah claimed. "You and me could be partners, Derek," said Dexter. Mrs. Rightover nicely picked up her apple and held it in her hand. She pretended that the class had just walked in when she started to sing….again.

"Let's start at the very beginning
The class must be quiet to start
When you read you begin with A-B-C
When you learn you begin by listening to me!
Mmm"

Before her song ended, the class was completely quiet.

Now that the class was back in order, Mrs. Rightover asked, "Are there any questions about the history project before I assign partners?" Hannah gladly raised her hand and asked, "Could you please give us some topics to choose from?" The class murmured, "Yea, that would be good." All eyes turned to Mrs. Rightover.

"Every group will get a sheet with names of most of the events in history up until now. But here are some events in history that are more popular: The signing of the Emancipation Proclamation, Independence Day, the day Ben Franklin discovered electricity, and the Civil Rights Movement."

Before Mrs. Rightover could say another word, Hannah had her hand raised again. "Yes, Hannah?" Mrs. Rightover asked. "Two people could pair up who are from different sides of town, like Teresa is from the Southside and I am from the Westside," Hannah suggested. Mrs. Rightover smiled and commented, "Thank you, Hannah. That is a good idea and I will keep that in mind." Hannah was surprised at Mrs. Rightover's answer.

What they did not know was that Mrs. Rightover had a book that had the addresses and phone numbers of each student. Holding the book behind her back, Mrs. Rightover said, "If there are no more questions, let me announce the names of each group."

The class became anxious. Everyone sat up and looked straight in front. Mrs. Rightover went through her roll book and started checking off names. In one final attempt to get Teresa as her partner, Hannah raised her hand and was about to speak when Mrs. Rightover stopped her. "Yes, Hannah. I remember what you suggested." Then with a small pause, Mrs. Rightover started announcing partners.

"Since the class has the same amount of boys and girls, there will be girl/boy groups." The class gave a sigh, "Ahh." Mrs. Rightover continued, "Susie you will work with Derek. Christina will partner with Dwayne. Teresa will work with Peter. Jennie will partner with James. Denise will work with Jacob. Cherry will partner with Martin." Hannah raised her hand and asked, "But who will I partner with, Mrs. Rightover?"

Mrs. Rightover smiled and said, "Oh, yes, Hannah. You will partner with Dexter." Dexter was just as surprised as Hannah. They both held their mouths open for at least five minutes.

"Each group will have 10 minutes to come up with their new history project idea," Mrs. Rightover announced. Hannah did not talk to Dexter and Dexter was not even interested in talking to Hannah. Five minutes passed before Mrs. Rightover realized that Hannah and Dexter were the only partners not talking. "Are you two going to do your history project or have you decided to get an F for the project?" asked Mrs. Rightover. They nodded their heads and shrugged. Refusing to accept their body language as an answer, Mrs. Rightover stated, "I don't understand head shakes, body language or shrugs, please speak to me." This was her way of getting students to talk to her.

At the same time, Hannah and Dexter answered, "Yes, ma'am. We are going to do our history project." Mrs. Rightover leaned over their desks and asked, "What event do you plan to do your project on?" Dexter spoke up first and said, "Well, we were going to cover the Civil Rights Movement of the 1960's." Hannah was not going to let Dexter get the credit for thinking of the history project idea. She immediately responded with, "I think we should do our project on the Holocaust of the 1940's."

Mrs. Rightover had an idea. "Since you can't seem to decide which event you want to explore, why not do a compare and contrast history project of both events. It will take longer hours of working together to complete, but you will both learn what each event means to one another," Mrs. Rightover declared.

Mrs. Rightover went to her desk and stated, "Remember class that each event in history must be thoroughly researched and those of you who have to review more than one event should put a combined effort in each event if you want a decent grade." One minute before the bell rang, she bellowed another tune that she continued to sing at the end of every class after that.

"So long, farewell, study hard tonight
I know you hate to leave this pretty sight
So long, farewell, study hard tonight
Goodbye, goodbye, good----bye."

When the bell rang, the class dispersed waving and singing— "goodbye," as they exited the classroom door. Mrs. Rightover's students seemed more peaceful and pleasant after they left her class. Her teaching style, singing and expectations caused her students to value themselves and others.

A week had passed before Hannah and Dexter finally agreed to meet at the Public Library to do their research. As they walked up the stairs, Hannah asked Dexter, "Do you think this project will take longer than our classmates'?" Dexter's response was, "I think so, because we have to write about two events and tell how they are the same and how they are different."

Their project did require longer hours to research each week than their classmates'. They agreed to work together and meet at the library an extra two hours a week to learn about the Civil Rights Movement and the Holocaust.

While at the Library, Hannah and Dexter asked each other questions to make sure they understood about both events. "Hannah, tell me what you know about the Holocaust." Hannah remarked, "The Holocaust is when millions of Jews were displaced, burned alive, put in gas chambers, and killed for no reason at all. Adolf Hitler, a dictator, was the leader during this awful time." Dexter wanted to know, "Why is the Holocaust so important to you?" She admitted, "It's important to me because my grandfather was a Jew during the 1940's and he barely survived the Holocaust. I am a Jew, too, and I don't want this to happen to anyone else ever again."

"So, Dexter, can you tell me about the Civil Rights Movement?" Dexter explained, "It all started when an African American woman named Rosa Parks refused to give up her seat on a bus to a Caucasian man. When she did not move, she was arrested and put in jail." Hannah interrupted, "Do you mean the law made a woman give up her seat to a man?" He continued, "Yes, Hannah. The laws said that this was allowed until a man named Martin Luther King Jr. came to help change these laws. He was kind, articulate and smart. So, he was named the leader of the Civil Rights Movement, which helped to bring fairness."

Three weeks went by and everyone in the class completed their projects. After Mrs. Rightover reviewed them all she announced, "It is obvious that each group spent time and effort on their history projects. I did not tell you that this project assignment was also a contest. The winning group will receive an all expense paid trip and will accompany me to Washington, DC in July."

Dexter pretended he did not care, but Hannah expressed great excitement about going to Washington, DC. Mrs. Rightover continued, "The winning group showed that working together can make a difference in understanding and appreciating another culture."

"The winners of the history project goes to the group that exhibited the most unity. Will Dexter and Hannah please come to the front of the class?" Mrs. Rightover asked. She smiled and handed them a large trophy as she read the inscription, "History Winners." Their names were engraved on the back: Dexter Baker and Hannah Maccabee. Both Hannah and Dexter smiled at each other and held up their trophy with great pleasure.

After class, they walked down the hallway together. Dexter said, "I sure am glad we won a trip to Washington, DC, because I want to be a politician when I grow up and I might get a chance to meet some politicians there." Hannah said, "I'm glad we won, because my father is there and I have not seen him since last summer."

This was the beginning of a new and different friendship for Hannah and Dexter. They soon forgot their first meeting and could only remember how they worked together to earn an A+ on their history project and win a free trip to Washington, DC. The singing, red-haired teacher had encouraged respect, cooperation, and academic achievement in two of the most unlikely partners in her class.

As a substitute for B's and C's, Hannah and Dexter aim for A's and B's. Instead of playing basketball everyday in the park and gossiping with their friends, Dexter visits the library twice a week and Hannah talks less about others and listens more to the facts.

You see, Hannah and Dexter were never the same again after their first meeting.

THE END